Published by Silver Press, Inc, P.O. Box 868, Windermere, FL
32786. Copyright © 1981 by Silver Press, Inc. All copyrights reserv-
ed. No part of this book may be reproduced in any form without
permission from the publisher. Printed in the United States of
America.

Library of Congress Cataloging in Publication Data

Chica.
    Celestine learns to swim.

    Translation of: Célestine apprend a nager.
    Summary: After Hubert accidentally falls
into the water, Celestine decides that they
both need swimming lessons.
    [1. Swimming—Fiction] I. Title.
PZ7.C4325Cef   [E]   81-14587
ISBN 0-86593-029-5   AACR2

Celestine
Learns to Swim

By Chica

Silver Press, Inc.
Windermere, Florida 32786

Celestine and Hubert had finished
washing their clothes.
"We will take them home now," said Celestine.

"Oh, I slipped on the soap," said Hubert.
"Watch out, the basket is turning over."

Hubert fell into the water.
"Help! I will drown," he yelled.

"Quick, grab my hand," said Celestine.

"There, I have you. You see, if you
could swim. . . . . ."
Celestine stopped talking. She was thinking.
"We will go home, Hubert. I have an idea,"
she said.

"Hello, is this the swimming coach? This is Celestine. Hubert and I want to learn to swim. We will be there tomorrow. We will learn to swim together."

"Oh, what funny swim suits," said Mr. Frog.
Mr. Frog was the swimming coach.

"He held them by two fishing poles, so
they would not drown.
He had them practice kicking and paddling.

"Look out, a monster!" cried Mr. Frog. "Swim for the dock! I will hold him off with this oar."

"I am afraid, Celestine," cried Hubert.
"Don't be afraid. I will help you," said Celestine.

"Take that, you Monster!" shouted Mr. Frog. Mr. Frog smashed the oar over the monster's head.

The pumpkin head smashed into a million pieces.
Everyone saw that it was not a monster, after all.
It was Charlotte, the turtle. She was playing
a trick on everyone.

"Oh, she is drowning!" yelled Mr. Frog.
Celestine dove into the water. Quickly,
she came up with Charlotte.

"Well done, Celestine!" everyone shouted.
"Hold her head above water."

Everyone helped to pull Charlotte out of the water.

They sat her in a chair. They made sure
that she was still breathing.

"I wanted to play a trick on you," said Charlotte.
"But, someone hit me so hard. Thank you for
diving into the water and saving me Celestine."

"Celestine can swim," said Mr. Frog.
"You are my best pupil."
Everyone was happy. They carried
Celestine on their shoulders.